Little Elephant
Thunderfoot

For the teachers and pupils
of the Richard Pate School

Dedicated to the work of Elefriends
S. G.

For Louise
J. B.

Published by
PEACHTREE PUBLISHERS, LTD.
494 Armour Circle NE
Atlanta, Georgia 30324

www.peachtree-online.com

Text © 1996 by Sally Grindley
Illustrations © 1996 by John Butler

First published by Orchard Books in Great Britain, 1996.

Printed in Hong Kong /China

10 9 8 7 6 5 4 3 2 1
First Edition

Library of Congress Cataloging-in-Publication Data

Grindley, Sally.
     Little Elephant Thunderfoot / Sally Grindley ; illustrated by John Butler. -- 1st ed.
          p.   cm.
          Summary: A baby elephant learns to feel secure with his grandmother, the head of the heard, until shots by poachers change his world.
          ISBN 1-56145-180-0
          1. Elephants--Juvenile fiction. [1. Elephants--Fiction. 2. Animals--Infancy--Fiction.] I. Butler, John, 1952–   ill.   II. Title.
PZ10.3.G886Li 1999
[E] --dc21   97-52591
                                                                                                                                        CIP
                                                                                                                                        AC

Little Elephant Thunderfoot

Sally Grindley

Illustrated by John Butler

PEACHTREE

ATLANTA

Little Elephant was only twenty minutes old but he knew he had to stand up. With one mighty effort, he gathered all four baggy gray legs beneath him and pushed. His head popped up above the undergrowth.

One more push and he was standing. He rocked unsteadily in the breeze.

Sunseeker, Little Elephant's mother, stood close by and guided him to her milk. He sucked hungrily, while Sunseeker ran her trunk gently over his body. Little Elephant felt warm and safe as he learned his mother's taste and smell.

Wise Old One was Little Elephant's grandmother and the head of the herd. She had roamed the savannah of southern Africa for fifty years. She was the eyes, the ears, and the trunk of the family. She showed them where to feed and where to play. She showed them where to find water, and what to do when danger was near.

Little Elephant was scared of his grandmother at first, because she looked so enormous. But Wise Old One was also very gentle, and Little Elephant soon loved to be close to her.

As Little Elephant grew bigger and stronger, he began to leave his mother's side. He played with his sisters, chasing through the long elephant grass. They lumbered along with wobbly heads and floppy trunks, kicking their legs out behind them, just for the fun of it.

Wise Old One called him Little Thunderfoot because he made so much noise.

It was a while before Little Thunderfoot found out what his trunk was for. It seemed to just wave around in front of his face. Then Wise Old One showed him how to touch and feel with it, and Little Thunderfoot liked putting the end in his mouth to try out different tastes.

Sometimes, he would playfully pull his grandmother's tail with his trunk, and she would butt him with her head.

Little Thunderfoot liked it best when Wise Old One led the family to the river. The elephants would rush into the water and wriggle and wrestle and splash.

When Little Thunderfoot dared to squirt Wise Old One with water, his grandmother would spray him back.

Then one day, when Little Thunderfoot was taking food from Wise Old One's mouth, she butted him away. He thought she was playing, but she stamped her foot and raised her head to listen. He shuffled away feeling puzzled. Wise Old One rumbled loudly. Something was wrong. She rumbled again and trumpeted.

Sunseeker and the other elephants heard her warning and quickly began to move off. Little Thunderfoot turned to follow. Suddenly there was a loud bang, followed by another, and Wise Old One fell to the ground.

When the elephants saw
Wise Old One fall, they stampeded.
Little Thunderfoot stared at his
grandmother and waited for her to
stand up and run with them, but
she didn't move. He went back and
touched her with his trunk, but still
Wise Old One didn't move.

Little Thunderfoot turned in fear and ran after his family. The elephants ran and ran, not really knowing where they were going. They just knew they had to get away. At last they found a safe place where dense thickets would protect them from danger.

The elephants pressed close together and touched each others' faces. They entwined trunks and rumbled and wheezed. They shook their heads and scratched the ground.

Frightened and confused, Little Thunderfoot pushed against Sunseeker for comfort. She stroked him with her trunk, but Little Thunderfoot sensed her panic. When would Wise Old One come and show them what to do?

When dawn broke, Sunseeker led her family back to where her mother still lay. She began to explore and caress every inch of Wise Old One's body with her trunk. Little Thunderfoot and the other elephants joined in. He could feel their sadness. His grandmother wasn't coming back.

They touched Wise Old One a last time. Then Sunseeker began to rip up clumps of grass and earth and throw them over her mother's body. Little Thunderfoot helped as best he could. He wanted his grandmother to be safe. It took all morning to cover her up.

Then Sunseeker led her family away. The elephants moved quickly, heading for the hills. Little Thunderfoot found it hard to keep up on his short, stubby legs. He was still just a baby.

They walked and walked for several days and nights. From time to time they stopped to listen and smell, their trunks held high to test the breeze. Little Thunderfoot grew tired and very hungry.

Then in the distance they saw another group of elephants.

Little Thunderfoot felt his mother's excitement push her sadness away for a brief moment. Sunseeker trumpeted loudly and charged triumphantly over to the group. With a great clacking of tusks, she greeted her sister, Earthwalker, and then leaned her head against her sister's side. Little Thunderfoot moved between them. Now he felt safe again.

Sunseeker and Earthwalker and their families stayed together. It was not easy for them without Wise Old One because she had known so much. But they helped each other along and as time passed each day became a little easier.

There were play times again, and bath times and fun times. But Little Thunderfoot would never forget his grandmother.

 Elefacts

Elephants, the largest land animals, are strong, intelligent, peaceful, and fun-loving. They can live for up to seventy years. A pregnant elephant carries her baby for nearly two years. As soon as the calf is born, it will stand up and begin to feed on its mother's milk.

The oldest female leads the herd, normally made up of daughters, granddaughters, sisters, and their offspring. They all help to look after the youngest elephants. The males grow up within the herd, but leave to live on their own when they are about sixteen years old. When a member of the herd dies, the other elephants often cover the body and mourn.

Elephants once roamed every landmass except Australia and Antarctica. They now live in the wild only in parts of southern Africa and in Asia. Their numbers have decreased partly because of the growth in human population and the loss of habitat, but mainly because of the illegal trade in elephant ivory.

Both the Asiatic and the African elephant are now listed as endangered species. To learn more about the conservation and protection of elephants, contact one of these organizations:
World Wildlife Federation, *www.worldwildlife.org,* 1-800-CALL-WWF, 1250 24th Street NW, Washington, DC 20077-7795
Wildlife Conservation International, New York Zoological Society, 185th Street & Southern Blvd, Bronx, NY 10460